BOOKS BY
JAMES HOWE

Bunnicula Books
Bunnicula
  (with Deborah Howe)
Howliday I nn
*The Celery Stalks at
  Midnight*
Nighty-Nightmare
Return to Howliday Inn
Bunnicula Strikes Again!
*Bunnicula Meets Edgar
  Allan Crow*

**Bunnicula and
  Friends**
The Vampire Bunny
Hot Fudge
Scared Silly
Rabbit-cadabra
The Fright Before Christmas

Picture Books
*There's a Monster Under
  My Bed*
*There's a Dragon in My
  Sleeping Bag*
Teddy Bear's Scrapbook
  (with Deborah Howe)
*Horace and Morris but
  Mostly Dolores*

*Horace and Morris Join
  the Chorus (but what
  about Dolores?)*
*Kaddish for Grandpa in
  Jesus' Name Amen*

**Tales from the
  House of Bunnicula**
*It Came from Beneath
  the Bed!*
*Invasion of the Mind
  Swappers from
  Asteroid 6!*
*Howie Monroe and the
  Doghouse of Doom*
*Screaming Mummies of
  the Pharaoh's Tomb II*
Bud Barkin, Private Eye
*The ~~Amazing~~ Odorous
  Adventures of Stinky Dog*

**Sebastian Barth
  Mysteries**
What Eric Knew
Stage Fright
Eat Your Poison, Dear
Dew Drop Dead

by JAMES HOWE

ILLUSTRATED BY LESLIE MORRILL

ALADDIN PAPERBACKS
New York London Toronto Sydney

This book is a work of fiction. Any references to historical events, real people, or real locales are used fictitiously. Other names, characters, places, and incidents are the product of the author's imagination, and any resemblance to actual events or locales or persons, living or dead, is entirely coincidental.

ALADDIN PAPERBACKS
An imprint of Simon & Schuster Children's Publishing Division
1230 Avenue of the Americas, New York, NY 10020
Text copyright © 1987 by James Howe
Illustrations copyright © 1987 by Leslie Morrill
All rights reserved, including the right of reproduction in whole or in part in any form.
ALADDIN PAPERBACKS and related logo are registered trademarks
of Simon & Schuster, Inc.
Also available in an Atheneum Books for Young Readers hardcover edition.
Manufactured in the United States of America
First Aladdin Paperbacks edition August 1997
This Aladdin Paperbacks edition August 2007
4 6 8 10 9 7 5
The Library of Congress has cataloged the hardcover edition as follows:
Howe, James.
Nighty-Nightmare.
"A Jean Karl book."
Summary: When scary strangers appear at the Monroes' overnight campsite, Chester the cat tries to convince the family's two dogs that foul play is intended.
ISBN-13: 978-0-689-31207-6 (hc)
ISBN-10: 0-689-31207-5 (hc)
[1. Camping—Fiction. 2. Cats—Fiction. 3. Dogs—Fiction.
4. Mystery and detective stories] I. Title.
PZ7.H83727Nk
1987 [Fic]—dc21 86022334
ISBN-13: 978-1-4169-3966-5 (pbk)
ISBN-10: 1-4169-3966-0 (pbk)
0909 OFF

To

MAUREEN HAYES—

Bunnicula's friend & mine

Contents

SOON AFTER THE PUBLISHING HOUSE for
which I work was purchased by a large manufac-
turer of computers and herbal soft drinks, I found
myself cleaning out my desk in preparation for a
move to new quarters. Feeling a little melancholy,
I was delighted to discover in the very bottom
drawer a manuscript of *Bunnicula, A Rabbit-Tale
of Mystery*. This was one of my first books as an
editor, and it brought back happy memories of the
afternoon its canine author, Harold X., appeared
at my door, the typewritten pages clenched in his
teeth.

I hadn't seen Harold in a long time, not since
before he'd hired a literary agent to handle his
affairs. Wondering what had become of him (and
eager to find out if he'd written anything since his
last book, *The Celery Stalks at Midnight*), I rang
up his agent, only to be informed by a machine
that she had given up her business to become a
yoga instructor. I replaced the receiver and wondered if I would ever see Harold again.

Gently I laid the manuscript at the top of the box of items I would personally move to my new office, reflecting once again on the changing times. You can well imagine my delight when a few days later I saw Harold's familiar face peek round the edge of my half-open door.

I dashed down the hall to the nearest vending machine, so we could celebrate our reunion over a chocolate bar. Happily I munched my half while reading the note accompanying Harold's new manuscript:

Dear friend,

My literary agent and I have parted ways. She wanted to call my new book Beyond the Further Adventures of Bunnicula: The Final Hare, or Terror in the Woods Part IV—The Book. *She said it would look great in paperback. Personally, I couldn't see it. In any event, shortly after she failed to sell the T-shirt rights to her latest best seller, she changed careers.*

Perhaps it is for the best. Now I can concentrate on writing without my mind being cluttered with commercial concerns. Knowing that you share with me a devotion to Literature, I hope you will find this latest effort worthy of your consideration.

> *Yours sincerely,*
> *Harold X.*

After Harold left, I pushed aside the fleeting thought that the title *Nighty-Nightmare* would look great on a sleepshirt and began to read.

ONE

The Adventure

IT BEGAN on the bottom of a canoe in the middle of Boggy Lake, some sixty miles from home and fifty yards from solid ground. The

gentle rocking of the boat was lulling me to sleep
when I felt Mr. Monroe's hand come to rest on
that spot between the tops of my ears where the
hair goes every which way and the scalp seems to
lie forever in wait for a little love and attention.
I sighed. Three pats usually led to some vigorous
scratching. But this time something was wrong.
Mr. Monroe didn't lift his hand after the second
pat. Instead, he left it there flat and heavy, like an
iron forgotten in the rush of attending to more
pressing matters.

I looked up, hoping to hear that he'd grown
tired of fishing and was ready to head back to the
cabin and cook up some s'mores. Ever since Toby
and Pete had introduced me to those gooey, crispy,
chocolaty delights the summer before, I couldn't
get enough. But s'mores were not what was on
Mr. Monroe's mind. Alas. No, he was in the mood
for reflection. And who better to share such moments, he was undoubtedly thinking, than man's
best friend himself?

"Harold," he said, staring off at the pine trees
along the lake's edge, "I'm going to be forty soon.

You know what that means, don't you?"

Birthday cake, I thought.

"It means half my life is over. Half my road is traveled. Half my songs are sung." I'd never thought about middle age that way before. Gee, I thought, half my naps are taken.

I whimpered sympathetically.

Mr. Monroe looked at me and smiled. "You understand what I'm talking about, don't you, ol' buddy?" In all the years I'd known him he'd never called me ol' buddy. I mean, he's a college professor. This was serious. "You know what we need? We need an adventure, Harold. We need to do something we've never done before. Something we always wanted to do in our youth but never did." I never chewed a chair leg, I thought. That would be fun. "Listen, boy, we're only here for a few days, but we still have time to do something new and adventurous and fun. Let's go on an overnight camping trip! We'll sleep out in the open, under the stars. What do you think, Harold?"

Mosquitoes, I thought. Ticks, I thought. Cockleburs. I wasn't sure I liked the idea at all. But then

something else occurred to me.

S'mores.

My tongue fell out of my mouth, and the next thing I knew I was looking into Mr. Monroe's eyes and drooling.

"That's the spirit, Harold," he said. "Let's go tell the others."

The paddle hit the water with a sharp smack. Mr. Monroe's eyes glinted with determination as he carried us quickly to shore. He wasn't simply homeward bound, however; he was bound for adventure, bound for recapturing his youth.

I had no idea then that he had set his course as well on what would prove to be the most terrifying night of my life.

TEN MINUTES LATER, we were at the door of "Lake Expectations," the Monroes' cabin retreat, named after Mr. Monroe's favorite book. The boys, who seemed to be the only ones around, came running when they heard their father call out his news. I couldn't help noticing that despite their enthusiasm, they managed to keep their tongues in their mouths.

"That is *so* cool," Pete shouted. "Can we go tonight?"

"Yeah, Dad, can we?" Toby echoed.

"I don't know," Mr. Monroe said as we all went inside. "I've never done this sort of thing before. There's a lot of preparation involved."

"Don't worry," said Pete. "I'll take charge."

"Well," his father said.

"No, its okay. Really," Pete said, in a tone I'd heard him using a lot lately. "I've been reading up on camping. For my badge, see. I know all about this stuff."

Mrs. Monroe came in from the back porch then, carrying a chipped pitcher full of buggy flowers. "Is this the secret project you've been working on?" she asked Pete.

Pete shook his head. "That's a different merit badge."

"Why can't you tell us about it?" Toby said.

"Because it's none of your business, squirt."

"Pete," said Mrs. Monroe, wiping the bottom of

the pitcher with her hand and placing it on the table.

"Well, it isn't fair," Pete said. "Toby thinks he has to do everything I do."

"I'm a scout, too," Toby said.

Pete looked at his younger brother and laughed. "You're a Bobcat," he said. "Anybody can be a Bobcat."

"Yeah, I guess so," Toby mumbled. "*You* were one once."

"Boys," said Mrs. Monroe. "Robert."

"Right," Mr. Monroe said. "If we're going to go on an overnight, let's have some fun doing it. I don't know what your other project is, Pete, but I see no reason why Toby can't help you out on this one. Why don't you get those camping books of yours, and we'll all pitch in? The sooner we're ready, the sooner we can leave."

"Yippee!" Toby shouted. "Can the animals come with us?"

"Oh, I don't know about *that*," Mrs. Monroe said. "They'll be fine here for one night."

"But they'll miss all the fun," Toby said. He

ran over and gave me a hug. "Harold wants to go, don't you, boy?" I licked his ear. "See?"

Mr. Monroe patted my head. Three times. And then he began to scratch. "This was Harold's idea almost as much as mine," he said. "I think he deserves to go."

"It's not Harold I'm worried about," Mrs. Monroe said. "It's the other two."

"Mom," said Pete, "there are three of them and four of us. They'll be okay. Really. Trust me." There was that tone again. It suddenly dawned on me that he used it only with his parents. He rarely yelled at them anymore; most of the time, he just smiled and spoke patiently, as if he'd discovered that they weren't as bright as they'd always let on. He seemed to be saying, "It's okay. Your secret is safe with me. I can handle making all the decisions from now on." I think this change occurred shortly after he turned eleven.

"Well, all right," Mrs. Monroe replied, "but four people for three animals is one person too many. *You* three are in charge of them."

"It's a deal," said Mr. Monroe.

Mrs. Monroe swatted at the bugs that had migrated from the pitcher of flowers to a nearby bowl of fruit. "I'll run to the store for supplies," she said, "while you fellas get the tents and sleeping bags in order. Do we even have a tent, Robert?"

Mr. Monroe looked blankly at his wife.

"No problem," said Pete. "Come on, Dad. I'll show you how to make a simple tent out of a tarp. We *do* have a tarp, don't we?"

Mr. Monroe looked blankly at his son.

I decided this would be a good time for me to leave. The family had their work cut out for them. And so did I. I had to break the news to Chester.

"Camping on Boggy Lake!?" Chester shouted, when I told him. "Didn't those bozos ever see *Friday the Thirteenth?*"

"I don't see what a stupid old horror movie has to do with real life," I said. Chester, being a cat, needs to have his reality checked from time to time, the way car owners have their oil checked.

Because he likes to read so much and watch all those movies on television, he's developed a reality leak that requires constant attention.

"Oh, you don't, eh?" he said, squinting in a knowing sort of way—or because the sun was in his eyes, I couldn't tell which. "Stories like that don't just materialize out of thin air, you know."

"*I* know that," I replied. Before I could say anything more, however, we were joined by Howie, who bounded up the steps of the back deck and practically knocked Chester over in his eagerness to be a part of the conversation.

"I know where stories come from, Pop," he said, gasping for air. Howie was usually out of breath. In fact, when he first came to live with us, less than a year ago, I was sure he suffered from some sort of bronchial ailment. But then I remembered what I'd been like as a puppy, and I realized he didn't have asthma after all. He was just young, and life was keeping him too busy to stop and catch his breath.

I saw that Chester's eyes were closed. It wasn't the sun; it was the effect of being called "Pop" by a *dog.* After all this time, he still wasn't used to it.

To keep the conversation moving, I asked, "Where do you think stories come from, Howie?"

"Big buildings," he said simply.

Even Chester had to open his eyes for this one.

"Don't you remember," Howie explained, "when we went to the vet two weeks ago, and we were all in the car, and Toby asked his father how many stories were in that new building downtown, and Mr. Monroe said fifteen, and there were five in the bank building, and seven in the insurance building and——"

"You're wanted on the telephone," Chester said.

"Really?" said Howie.

"Yes. Hurry inside. It's important."

Howie didn't say another word but padded off quickly on his little dachshund legs through the back door into the kitchen.

Chester must have seen my look, because he said right away, "Spare me the lecture on cruelty to children, Harold. If I hadn't found a way to stop him, he'd have gone on forever. And we don't have forever. We have to talk about this camping trip the Monroes are planning."

"It's nice you're so worried about them, Chester, but—"

"It's not *them* I'm worried about. It's *us*. They're taking us with them, Harold. Thanks to you and your little heart-to-heart with Mr. Monroe."

"I couldn't help it," I said. "I pictured us all around the campfire, toasting marshmallows, singing songs. 'Someone's in the kitchen with Dinah, someone's in the kitchen, I know-oh-oh-oh. Someone's in the kitchen with Di-*nah*—' "

"Listen, Harold," Chester said, just as I was getting to the part about the banjo, "while someone's in the kitchen with Dinah, have you thought about who's in the woods with *us*?"

"What do you mean?"

"The woods are full of spirits."

"What woods?"

"Any woods. They're dark places, Harold, harboring evil creatures who prey on the innocent."

"Do the Boy Scouts know about this?" I asked.

Chester ignored me and went on. "This time of

year is the worst. 'The fifth of May is Saint George's Day. When midnight tolls, the devil has sway.' "

"That's pretty good," I said. "I wrote a poem once."

"I didn't write that. I read it in a book."

"Oh-oh."

"I'm serious, Harold. This camping trip can only mean trouble."

Just then, the screen door squeaked open, and Howie popped out. "Boy, this camping trip is going to be fun," he said, running toward us. "You should see all the neat stuff they're doing in there, Uncle Harold. First Pete was showing his father how to sharpen his knife, and now he's teaching him first aid. It's lucky Mr. Monroe is right-handed."

"The first blood," Chester muttered.

"What'd you say, Pop?"

"Chester didn't say anything," I said. "Who called?"

"What?"

"Who wanted you on the phone?"

"Oh, nobody important. Just one of those surveys. They wanted to know which dog food I like best."

Chester's eyes widened. "I worry about you sometimes," he said to Howie, and he walked away. I knew what he meant. The Monroes don't have a telephone at the cabin.

Howie went off to play, and I went around to the front of the house to find some sun. I settled in on the front porch, napping for the next hour or so. Chester's worries were the furthest thing from my mind, and I probably wouldn't have thought of them again at all if it hadn't been for the newspaper Mrs. Monroe brought back with her from the store. As she was opening the door to the cabin, the paper fell out of her bag and landed a few inches from my nose.

It wasn't the headline that caught my eye. It was the date: May 4.

We would be in the woods at midnight. Midnight of Saint George's Day.

Two Men
and a Dawg

SOMEHOW, DESPITE Mr. Monroe's bumbling and Chester's mumbling, we managed to get on our way by about four o'clock that afternoon. I know the time because that's when my stomach alarm goes off to remind me I have two hours until my next meal. In case I get distracted, a second alarm goes off around five so I can begin panicking. That day, however, I decided to start my panicking a little early. On a camping trip, I had no idea *when* I'd be fed. As it turned out I didn't have to worry about it. But my panicking wasn't in vain. It was good practice for everything that happened later.

I also needn't have worried about ticks and mosquitoes. By the time we'd driven to the other side of the lake and were finally out in the woods, I'd been covered with so much spray that only bugs wearing gas masks could have gotten through. Howie, Chester, and I kept our distance from one another and the rest of the Monroes. It was hard to avoid the smell, though; in fact, I half expected the entire family to be picked up at any minute on charges of polluting the air.

"I don't think *anybody* has ever been *this* way before," Pete shouted out.

"A comforting thought," I heard Chester mutter. I knew what Pete was saying wasn't so, but I didn't mention it then. I may not have done a lot of tracking in my life, but I knew enough to tell that someone *had* been this way before—and not so long before, either.

"Don't worry, son," Mr. Monroe shouted back.

"I'm not worried, Dad. I think it's cool. Maybe if we're lucky, we'll get lost and I can save us."

"*I* have a compass," Toby said.

"*I* have a compass and a map," Pete said. "And if anybody chokes I can do the Heimlich maneuver."

"I hope that isn't a requirement for one of your badges," Mr. Monroe said.

Personally, I took Pete's remark as a hopeful one. You have to eat before you can choke, after all.

Howie, meanwhile, didn't seem to have a worry in the world. He was sniffing the air happily, ignoring the stench of insect repellent for the more delicious and inviting aromas in the air. "Smell those pine trees!" he cried. "Smell those wild flowers! Smell that smoke!"

Smoke?

Suddenly, Mrs. Monroe, who with Toby was in the lead, stopped in her tracks and pointed. "Look," she called back to her husband.

Pete and Mr. Monroe ran to catch up with the others. The three of us were quick to follow.

"Someone's camping over there by the lake," Mrs. Monroe said. "They already have a fire going.

I think we should head in that direction."

"Oh, Mom," Pete said, "we don't want to make camp near somebody else. The whole idea of this is to go it alone."

"No, the whole idea is to get through the night. So far, no one," and she glanced at her husband's bandaged hand, "has demonstrated a reassuring flair for survival."

"We have Pete's books," Mr. Monroe said tentatively.

"Better than that," said their oldest son. "You have *Pete*."

"You haven't earned that merit badge yet," said Mrs. Monroe. "Look, I don't want to argue about this. If no one else were around, I'd say let's just pitch our tent wherever we end up. But the point is, there *is* someone else around, and I'll bet they know a lot more about camping than we do."

Pete and Toby looked to their father.

"Your mother is right," he said. "It can't hurt to have somebody nearby."

"It can if that somebody is a homicidal maniac," Chester whispered to me.

"Sshh," I said, not wanting Howie to overhear.

Howie, however, had already run on ahead of us, sniffing at the ground as he went. When we caught up with him he asked, "Is this how you track, Uncle Harold? Am I doing it right?"

"That's right," I said. "Just put your nose to the ground and follow it."

"Makes scents to me," he said with a chuckle. "Get it, Uncle Harold? Get it, Pop? It makes *scents* to me."

I chuckled back. Chester just rolled his eyes and commented, "Let's hope you'll still be laughing at midnight, Harold."

Behind us, the Monroes were singing as they walked. It was a silly song about a bunny rabbit, one I hadn't heard in a long time, and it got me thinking about Pete and Toby when they were little. But then, as I listened to the words, I started thinking about someone else.

"It's too bad," I remarked to Chester, "that Bunnicula couldn't have come camping with us. He always gets left out of these adventures we have."

"Yeah," Howie said. "Just because he's a rabbit, I don't see why he has to stay home in his cage all the time."

"Rabbits don't understand camping trips," Chester said. "If Bunnicula were here, he'd go brainlessly hopping this way and that, and the next thing you know, he'd be lost."

"That would be terrible," Howie said sadly.

"Darn right it would," said Chester. "Can you just imagine *him* lost in the woods? I can see the headlines now—'Evergreen Forest Turns White!'"

"Here we go again," I said.

"Besides, a vampire rabbit," Chester went on, "is the last thing we need with us on Saint George's Day."

"Saint George's Day?" Howie asked. "What's that?"

"Nothing," I said quickly.

"Stop protecting the kid," Chester said. And then, before I could say another word, he told Howie all about the evil spirits and the woods and midnight.

[26]

Howie's eyes grew larger and larger and larger. "I want to go home," he whimpered when Chester was through.

"Howie," I said, "Chester is telling stories out of books. Nothing like that is going to happen here. There's no evil in these woods. There is *nothing* to be scared of."

"Oh, really?" said Chester, coming to a sudden halt.

Straight ahead of us, not ten feet away, were two men and a dog. One man was frying some fish over an open fire. I couldn't see his face, but his hands made me think of spiders. The hairs rose a little along the back of my neck. They rose even higher when I glanced at the other man sitting on a rock nearby. His head was the shape of a potato, all lumpy and swollen. His right eye twitched. And in his hands he held a large knife. He wasn't doing anything with it, just holding it. From time to time, he'd turn it over, and then he'd spit on the ground.

The dog, also potatolike, sat by his feet. He didn't look as if he had the energy to spit. A long ribbon of drool hung from his lower lip, as much a part of him as the scar that ran across his jowl.

When the Monroes arrived right after us, the man by the fire looked up.

"Well, howdy," he said. "You folks out camping?"

"We . . . we thought we'd camp over there," Mrs. Monroe said, pointing to a sandy patch near the water's edge. "That is, if you don't mind."

"Mind? Heck, no. We never do get to see people in these parts. I'm Bud. And that there is Spud."

Spud, I thought. How fitting.

The Monroes introduced themselves and us. Spud looked everybody over, turned the knife in his hands, and spat on the ground.

"Nice-looking animals you got there," Bud said, wiping his hands on the back of his jeans. "Yes'm. Nice looking. Now, you take Dawg, he's seen better days. He cain't help it, he's been kicked around by life, and sometimes he jes gets downright mean and orn'ry. But he's a good dawg, Dawg is."

"That's your dog's name?" said Mr. Monroe. "Dog?"

"Dawg," said Bud.

He flipped the fish in the frying pan. Spud spat. Dawg dragged himself to his feet and, drool and all, headed in our direction.

"He looks a little like Max," I commented, trying to cheer myself by bringing to mind a friendly bulldog of our acquaintance.

"Yeah, the way a rattler looks like a garter snake. Happy Saint George's Day," Chester said, and the hairs continued to rise all the way down my back.

"What kind of mutt do you call yourself?" Dawg growled as he came closer. His teeth were stained and pitted like old linoleum.

"Nonviolent," I said, hoping he wouldn't catch the tremor in my voice.

He snorted, sending a waft of rancid breath my way, and started to circle me, sniffing. If there's one thing I can't stand, it's this humiliating sniffing routine that passes for a handshake in the dog world. I would have suggested that he "give me five," but I was a little too nervous. Besides, I didn't have the feeling Dawg was the kind of old dog who was keen to learn new tricks. In fact, I didn't have the feeling Dawg was too keen at all.

"Watch this," he said, when he'd tired of sniffing. He sauntered over to the campfire, stopping only when he was so close that his mangy fur took on a red glow. I exchanged puzzled glances with Chester and Howie, wondering what it was we were supposed to be watching.

The Monroes, meanwhile, had moved down the slope to their campsite. Bud, who had gone back to his fish, ignored Dawg, while Spud just stared off into space, slowly turning his knife in his hands. After a moment, Dawg barked. The two men looked up and Bud started to shout, "Lookee, Spud. *Hot* dawg! *Hot* dawg!" His wild laughter made him sound like a demented goose. From the way Dawg and Spud curled their lips, I gathered that this was meant to be a big joke. Suddenly, I had the feeling I knew how prehistoric cavemen might have entertained themselves. I decided maybe television wasn't such a bad invention after all.

"Gee, Uncle Harold," Howie said, "What do you think?"

"I think Chester's right," I replied. "The woods are full of spirits tonight."

"Evil spirits?"

"*Stupid* spirits," I said.

Chester mumbled something, but I couldn't hear him over the sound of the can opener in the distance. Dinner was about to be served, and I wasn't going to miss it.

AFTER I'D EATEN, while Toby and Pete and Mr. Monroe renewed their attempts at keeping the family's improvised tent upright, I joined Howie and Chester for a stroll along the lake's edge.

"This isn't so bad, is it, Chester?" I said. "It's a beautiful night. The moon will be out soon."

"It's a *full* moon tonight," Chester commented.

"I'm full, too," said Howie.

"Listen to the water lapping the shore," I suggested.

"Watch where you step," Chester countered. "You never know what's been washed up."

"The trouble with you, Chester, is that you've lost your capacity to enjoy the simple things in life."

"That isn't true," Chester replied. "I enjoy you."

"Thank you." I sighed deeply. "The world is full of wonder," I said. I often get philosophical after meals. "Behold its majesty. Marvel at its creatures great and small."

"Not to mention weird," said Chester. He nodded toward a figure sitting on its haunches several yards ahead of us. I could tell from the potatolike silhouette that it was Dawg.

He was looking out at the horizon, waiting for sunset, perhaps, or dreaming of sunsets past. When we approached, he shared his thoughts with us. "You could spit till you're dry," he said, "and never make a lake."

Chester hissed, a cat's way of booing.

"You come here often?" I asked Dawg, hoping to compensate for Chester's lack of good manners.

"Cheez," Chester said under his breath, "why don't you ask him his sign?"

"Not so often," said Dawg, apparently oblivious to Chester's rude remark. "Bud and Spud, they . . . they don't get out much."

"Well," Chester said, loudly enough for Dawg to hear this time, "it was certainly nice of the warden to let them out for Saint George's Day."

There was a glimmer in Dawg's eyes. Of a pretty low wattage, mind you, but a glimmer nonetheless. "Saint George's Day," he said. "Funny you should mention that."

"Funny?" said Chester. "What strikes you as funny?"

"Just before we came here, Bud said something about it being a special day soon. He said . . . he said. . . ."

The glimmer faded, and I wondered how long we'd have to wait for the bulb to be changed. " 'He said?' " I prompted hopefully.

"He said," Dawg went on, "that this was the night to find it."

"Find it?" Howie squealed. He was beginning to shiver a little, as the wind coming off the lake turned colder. I felt a chill go through me, too. "Find what?"

"I don't know," said Dawg. "He didn't say. But I do know one thing. Bud'll find it, and Spud'll know what to do with it."

A sudden *whiz* and *thunk* grabbed our attention. In the distance, Spud walked to a tree and pulled his knife from where it had lodged.

"Oh, yeah," Dawg said. "Spud'll know what to do, all right."

THREE

Things Are Not What They Seem

" 'SOMEONE'S in the kitchen with Di-*nah*, strummin' on the old banjo. And singin', fee-fie, fiddly-eye-oh. Fee-fie, fiddly-eye-oh-oh-oh-oh. . . .' "

Hearing the Monroes' voices raised in song, seeing the warm glow on their faces, watching them sharpen their sticks in preparation for marshmallow treats, I was content. It had been only ten minutes since Dawg had made his ominous remark at the water's edge, ten minutes since I'd felt the cold wind run through me, but all that might as well have happened in another lifetime. For now

there was nothing more on my mind than peace
on earth, good will to men, and the unopened bag
of marshmallows lying at Toby's side.

"Listen to the happy campers," Chester said of
the Monroes. I glanced over my shoulder to where
he lay stretched out on a log, the firelight dancing
in his eyes. "How innocent they are in their merry-
making. While out there somewhere in the shadows of the night—"

"It isn't dark yet," I observed.

"In the woods it is always dark," he said. "In the forest of the soul it is always night."

"Chester," I said, "have you been reading Stephen King again?"

"Howdy, folks."

I was spared a book report by the arrival of Bud, Spud, and the inevitable Dawg.

"Well, hello, Bud," Mr. Monroe said. "We were just about to toast some marshmallows. Would you and your brother care to join us?"

Bud smiled awkwardly, as if he'd long been out of practice. "Why, sure, that'd be right nice. That fire isn't going to last long, though. Who made that thang?"

Pete cried, "I did!"

"Well, I don't know who taught ya about fires, young fella, but that one's got about as much life in it as a toad what's jes shook hands with a steamroller."

"I'm a Boy Scout of America," Pete said proudly. "I learned how to make a fire from the Fieldbook."

"Page one seventeen," Toby said, coming to his brother's defense.

"You cain't build a fire from a book," Bud scoffed. "I'll get that thang goin' again in no time. Say, I tell you what. It isn't going to get dark for another twenty minutes or so. Why don't you-all go for a walk along the crick? There's a purty falls up there. You folks know this part of the lake?"

"We've never been here before. We have a cabin cross t'other side," said Mr. Monroe, looking as surprised as the rest of us at what had come out of his mouth. I wondered if it was just a matter of time before we were all saying "thang" and "howdy."

"Well, now, Spud knows these parts like he knows his own name," said Bud. "He can git you up Latawata Crick to Breakneck Falls afore dark. And by the time you get back, I'll have this fire going good and strong."

I saw Mrs. Monroe exchange a worried look with her husband. "I don't know," she said. "It's getting late. Our boys should be in bed soon."

"Oh, Mom," Toby whined. "We go to bed later than this at home."

"Yeah," Pete said. "We have to toast marsh-mallows yet and sing some more songs."

"And tell scary stories," said Toby. "We *can't* go to bed until we tell scary stories."

"The boys are right," Mr. Monroe said. "This is meant to be an adventure. And you don't go to bed early on an adventure. Come on, Ann, let's go." He reached out his hand, which Mrs. Monroe reluctantly accepted. "What do you say, boys," he said, turning to us, "how about a little exercise? Harold, with the way you've been eating lately, you could stand to lose a pound or two."

I tried to ignore Howie's chuckling as I struggled to my feet. Dawg came over. "You're going to like Breakneck Falls," he informed us. "One hundred feet of falling water."

"For you droolers and spitters on our tour," Chester said, "here's one sight you won't want to miss."

"I have the feeling yer friend is making wise at my expense," Dawg said with a snarl. "If he is, he'd better watch out."

"Threats don't frighten me," said Chester.

"Well," Dawg said, as the light from Spud's knife glanced off the fire in our direction, "there's more than one way to skin a cat."

"Spud," Bud shouted. "Spud, take these folks up to the falls. Spud. Spud, I'm talking to *you*."

As we set off, Chester turned to Howie and me and said, "How comforting to think that Spud knows these parts like he knows his own name."

NOW THE TRUTH of the matter is that had it not been for Mr. Monroe's crack about my weight, I might never have taken that hike. Vanity, thy name is flab. I consoled myself that having worked off an astonishing number of calories, I would be entitled to an extra portion of s'mores on my return. But as I traveled the wet and buggy path up Latawata Creek, I began to worry. Not about s'mores, but about the night itself. I don't know if it was Spud's silence, which spread like contagion among the Monroes, or the unfamiliar sounds of the forest, but something was definitely beginning to spook me.

By the time we'd reached Breakneck Falls, I was too unnerved by the creatures I'd begun to imagine lurking behind every tree along the way to care much about its beauty. My lack of enthusiasm disappointed Dawg, and I suspect I have no one to blame but myself for the trouble that ensued after I commented to that effect.

"Ain't that a sight?" said Dawg.

"Wow," Howie uttered breathlessly.

"Not bad," Chester remarked.

"It reminds me," I said, "of the time Pete left the water running in the upstairs tub."

"That all?" said Dawg. "Then I'll show you something that will *really* impress you. Follow me."

He bounded off through the woods. Without thinking, Howie and I bounded off after him.

"Come on, Pop!" Howie cried over his shoulder.

I saw Chester looking back and forth between us and the Monroes.

"Come back!" Mr. Monroe was calling.

"Harold!" Mrs. Monroe shouted. "Howie come here!"

Spud spoke then, for the first time. "Don't worry about them," he said. "Dawg knows his way around these woods like he knows his own name."

Spud might have said something else then or maybe it was the glint of his knife as he pulled it from his belt that did it, but the next thing I knew, Chester was behind us.

When we caught up with Dawg at last, there was just enough daylight left to see that we were in a clearing of some sort, surrounded on all sides by tangled trees and vines.

"Dawg," I said, catching my breath.

He regarded me with a vacant stare.

"Dawg?"

"Actually, Dawg is my nickname," he said then. "My real name is Teufel. It's German."

"What does it mean?" I asked.

"I know," Chester said, as the last remaining

NIGHTY-NIGHTMARE

light fell away and there was no one left in the stillness of the place but the four of us and the shadows. "It means . . . *'devil.'* "

"Oh," I said, "should we call you Teufel?"

"No, no, Dawg's jes fine. I wanted to clear up my real name, that's all."

"Things are not what they seem," Chester said to me. Then to Dawg, he said, "Well, as long as you're clearing things up, where is . . . whatever it is you wanted us to see?"

"Well, that's hard to say," Dawg said.

"Wh-where are we?" Howie asked, starting to whimper.

"Oh, now, that's easy," said Dawg. "We're lost."

FOUR

Nobody Here But Us Chickens

"LOST ? ! ! " CHESTER SHRIEKED.
With that, Howie's whimpering quickened by several rpm's. I decided the last thing an impressionable young puppy needed at the moment was hysteria.

"Chester," I said, "calm down. Dawg knows these woods like he knows his own name. Right, Dawg? Dawg. Dawg, I'm talking to *you*." A whimper started to rise in my throat. "Well," I said, swallowing it, "at least there's a full moon,

so it should be easy enough to find our way back to camp."

Just then, a cloud passed over the moon.

"Aw, you guys are so lily-livered," Dawg said. "You'd think these woods was full of ghosts er something."

"Er something," said Chester.

"May-maybe we *should* go back to camp," Howie suggested.

Dawg sidled up to Howie. "Whatsa matter?" he said. "You chicken?"

"No, sir!" Howie said. "We're not chicken, are we, Uncle Harold?"

"Of course not," I said. "It's just—"

"We're not chicken, are we, Pop?" Howie asked Chester.

"Buck-buck-buck-*buck*!" Chester cackled.

This made Howie laugh. "That was pretty funny," he said. "You're a regular *Hen*-ny Young-man, Pop."

Chester scowled.

"Who's Henny Youngman?" I asked.

"An old-time comedian," Chester said. "Howie's been listening to Mr. Monroe's nostalgia tapes again."

"Yep, that was pretty funny," Howie went on. "Just watch out that your next joke doesn't lay an *egg,* though." He chortled merrily, having forgotten our predicament, it seemed.

Dawg took advantage of the situation. "Come on, Howie," he said, "what do you say? I'll show you what I wanted to show you and get you back to camp before you know it."

"All *right*!" Howie shouted. "Let's go!"

"I thought we were lost," Chester pointed out.

"Well, we are," Dawg replied. "So at least we don't have to worry about that anymore."

"Makes sense," I said, as we started off.

"Something else is beginning to make sense," Chester whispered to me. We were trailing several yards behind Dawg and Howie.

"What?" I asked.

"Dawg wants us lost."

"Oh, come on, Chester," I said. "Why would he want that?"

"I don't know, but there's something fishy about this whole thing. I think he's leading us somewhere, Harold. Leading us to our doom."

"Well, at least we've eaten," I said, trying to humor Chester out of his gloomy thoughts.

"Our last meal, perhaps," Chester mumbled. And then he stopped dead in his tracks.

"What's wrong?" I asked.

"I've figured it out," he said. "The Monroes, they—"

"What?" I said, beginning to feel alarmed. Chester has a way of doing that to me at times.

"Don't you see, Harold? He's leading us on a wild goose chase so that the Monroes will be alone with—"

"Bud and Spud," I said, finishing the sentence for him.

"Harold, the Monroes are in danger."

"You could be right," I said. "Bud suggested we take this hike. And Spud didn't try to stop us when we took off after Dawg. But what can we do now? We don't know our way back."

"We'll have to look for an opportunity to break away from Dawg," Chester said. "Then you and Howie can put your tracking skills to good use."

I looked ahead. Howie was racing to keep up with Dawg, laughing as he went.

"I think Howie has made a friend," I remarked to Chester.

"A calculated move on Dawg's part," he said. "He's won an ally. He knows we won't leave

Howie behind. And now we'll have a hard time convincing Howie of Dawg's ill intentions. Oh, Harold, I believe we underestimated the moronic mutt. He's no dummy, after all."

Dawg turned back. "You guys coming or are you going to flap yer yaps all night?" he yelled. The moonlight made the ribbon of drool hanging from his lower lip glisten. It reminded me of Spud's knife shining in the light of the Monroes' campfire.

But then I noticed once again the vacant look in his eyes.

"I don't know, Chester," I said. "It's difficult to imagine Dawg as being capable of what you're suggesting."

When we were still lost three hours later, it had gotten easier.

FIVE

Nighty-Nightmare

MY LEGS ACHED from walking. I'd never realized just how *big* the woods were on this side of Boggy Lake. Was Dawg trying to wear us down, so that when we finally stopped to sleep, there would be no fear of our waking until it was all over? I tried not to think such thoughts but couldn't help myself. With each step we took, with each utterance Chester made about the spirit of evil being let loose at midnight, with each reflection of the moon I caught in Dawg's eyes, I wondered . . . and I wondered . . . and I wondered.

"What do you suppose is happening to the Monroes?" I asked at one point. Chester just shook his head darkly, and I didn't ask again.

After a time, he began telling stories of Saint George's Day, not to frighten us, he assured me under his breath, but to check out Dawg's reactions. There were none that were noticeable. Howie, seeing the lack of response in Dawg, reacted not out of fear but delight.

"Tell us more," he'd say after Chester had finished each tale of twilight terror.

And so Chester would regale us with another.

And another.

Until: "It is near," he said. And he fell silent.

I believe he was referring to the midnight hour. But Dawg interpreted his remark differently.

"Yep," Dawg said. "We're going in the right direction this time. I can feel it. Pretty soon, we'll be there."

"I can't wait," Howie squealed enthusiastically, as if we'd been walking for three minutes rather than three hours.

Dawg sniffed at the ground. "If we just follow the bed of this stream," he said, "we'll be there right quick."

We walked now on muddy ground, our paws sticking with each step. Covered with cockleburs and mud, I was beyond the point of caring, wanting only to stop and rest, stop and sleep for the night . . . even if it meant the worst. I was beginning to nod off, when I heard Howie's excited voice cry out, "Look! Look, there in the mud!"

Chester, Dawg, and I rushed to Howie's side. There were fresh footprints.

"The prints of darkness," Howie said ominously.

"They were made by people," Dawg said. "I wonder if that means . . . yep, I'll bet it does. We're almost there, just like I told ya. Come on, follow me!"

Once again, he bounded off. Howie, who was as endlessly full of energy as a rechargable battery, was quick to follow. Chester and I lagged behind.

By the time we caught up with them, they had found what Dawg had been looking for all this time. Through an opening in the trees, we made out a large house standing in an open field. Its spires were silhouetted against a purple sky; its windows were dark but for one, which quivered with a yellow light. It seemed like something from another time and place.

When he saw it, Chester gasped.

"I'll bet you never thought you'd see *that* in the middle of the woods," Dawg said. "Ain't it a sight?"

"It looks like a castle," said Howie.

"Or a cathedral," I said.

We turned to Chester for his response, but there was none—none other than the look of sheer horror on his face, that is.

"Come on," Dawg said, "let's go closer."

"No!" Chester cried.

"Aw, come on," said Dawg, "don't start that chicken stuff again."

"It . . . it isn't that," Chester stuttered. He looked up at the sky. It had grown cloudier, but the light of the moon was still strong and full of power. "I'm tired, that's all. I think maybe we should go back to camp. Do you know the way, Dawg?"

Dawg frowned. "Well, shore, but don't you wanta see the house? We've come all this way." He turned to Howie and yawned in spite of himself. "You wanta see it, don't you, Howie?"

"He's stalling," Chester whispered to me. "We've got to get back to camp. We don't have much time till midnight. And the last thing we

want to do is go near that house. Anywhere but *that* house."

"Why?" I asked. "What are you talking about?" But Chester couldn't answer, because Dawg and Howie were looking to us for a decision.

"I don't know about you, but I'm beat," Chester said. "What do you say we try to get some rest? Then we can go see the house, and *then* go back to camp."

Dawg yawned again. "Well, okay," he said. "I wouldn't mind setting down these weary bones for a spell. It looks like there's some shelter over there under those leaves. Is this all right with you, little fella?"

Howie stretched his mouth wide, trying to make his yawn as big as Dawg's, I think. "Sure," he said.

As we settled in, I tried not to be hurt by the fact that Howie cuddled up to Dawg's side instead of mine. Chester didn't allow me any time for hurt feelings, however. "As soon as Dawg is asleep," he whispered, "we grab Howie and run.

"Nighty-night," he said to Dawg and Howie, who were curled up several feet away from us.

"Nighty-night," Howie said.

Dawg grumbled something I couldn't make out. It might have been "nighty-night," but garbled in some unidentifiable, macho way.

Well, I thought, as I looked up through the leaves at the broken pattern of stars and clouds above me, here I am: middle-aged and having an adventure. It wasn't quite what I'd had in mind when Mr. Monroe had suggested an overnight camping trip, but I was sleeping under the stars and there was no denying that an adventure was what I was having. I wondered about Mr. Monroe then. What kind of adventure was he having? I shuddered as I thought about it and wondered how long it would take for Dawg to go to sleep.

Looking in his direction, I saw his eyes shining in the dark. It seemed the moon was forever reflected in them. He blinked when he saw me looking at him. I swallowed hard.

"Having trouble sleeping?" I asked.

"I always do," he said. "This ol' body of mine's

got so many breaks and bruises in it that something's always aching. Don't worry about me, I'll just rest while you all sleep. I don't mind."

"Great," Chester muttered. Then to Dawg, he said, "Would anything help you sleep?"

Dawg thought for a moment. "A doggie-bone softened in warm milk," he said at last. I was ready to forgive him anything when he said it, but then it occurred to me that even Al Capone, the most notorious gangster of them all, probably liked his milk and cookies now and again.

"Well, we're a little short on milk," Chester said. "How about a lullaby? Harold, sing him the song about Dinah in the kitchen. Soft and low, Harold. Soft and low."

I was about to open my mouth in song, when the words froze in my throat. There was someone out there. I heard the crackling of branches, voices whispering in the dark. "Chester, did you hear?" I hissed.

"Of course," Chester said. "The evil spirits are waking to the devil's alarm. Midnight is upon us.

The sooner we get this clown to sleep, the better. Sing, Harold."

I opened my mouth again, but was stopped this time by Dawg. "To tell you the truth," he said, "what would help me to sleep better than a song is a story."

"Yeah," Howie said, "that's what we need. A story. Just think, if we were back at the campfire with the Monroes, we'd be telling ghost stories. Tell us a ghost story, Pop."

"Well, I don't know," Chester said. The leaves about us stirred in the wind. A branch snapped somewhere off to my left.

"A scary story," Dawg said. "Yer good at that, Chester. If you want me to go to sleep, you'd better tell me a scary story." His words sounded like a threat, like he knew that we knew. If you *want* me to go to sleep, he'd said.

I looked to Chester, whose eyes were focused on the house in the distance. The quivering yellow light faded and went out. The house was dark and still. "All right," Chester said, "I'll tell you a story. A story of Saint George's Day. A true story. One that started in Transylvania and ended right here."

"Here?" I said, feeling my hair begin to rise. Boy, my hair was really getting a work out tonight.

"It is the history of a vampire rabbit named Bunnicula," Chester went on. "The little-known but true story of a race of creatures who brought terror wherever they roamed and passed on to each generation the secrets of their evil ways."

"I get it," said Howie. "This is the story of a hare with dark roots."

SIX

Once Upon a Time in Transylvania

CHESTER TOOK A MOMENT to bathe his tail. Howie, Dawg, and I settled down on our bed of pine needles and leaves and waited. The air that ruffled our hairs and rustled the trees above us was changing, perhaps in anticipation as well, though anticipation of what, I couldn't say. When Chester was ready to begin, he assumed the classic cat position—head high, spine erect, front legs as straight and formal as marble columns—and wrapped his freshly laundered tail around himself, leaving only the tip in motion. For a time, it flicked

the ground. Then slowly it quieted. And the story began.

"Once upon a time in Transylvania," Chester said, "high in the Carpathian Mountains in a little town called Kasha-Varnishkes, there lived twin brothers, whose names were Hans and Fritz. The simple sons of simple innkeepers, their lives were—"

"Simple?" I ventured.

"Free from care," said Chester. "Free from worry. Until that fateful day when everything changed. 'Wash up for dinner,' their mother told them, as she did every night before the evening meal. 'Going, Mummy,' said Fritz, the more obedient of the two. 'Take your brother with you,' their mother said."

"Well, sure," Howie put in. "After all, you don't want dirty Hans at dinner."

Chester sighed deeply and continued. "They were just going outside to the well when they heard a crash. Rushing back in, they found their mother lying in a heap on the floor. 'Mummy!' Fritz cried."

"This Fritz is a real wimp," Dawg muttered. I tended to agree, though I said nothing.

" 'Is she dead?' said Hans. 'No,' Fritz told his brother. 'But I think she's had a relapse. Oh, Hans, you know what we were told the last time this happened. There is only one doctor, a doctor in far-off London, who can cure her. What are we to do? We are the poor children of poor innkeepers. So few people pass by this way, it will take us years to save enough money to go to London and get help. And Mummy doesn't have years.' Fritz began to cry.

"Feeling her son's teardrops on her lips, the woman blinked open her eyes. 'Is that you, Stefan?' she said. Hans and Fritz looked sadly at each other. 'Mummy, you know that Papa is gone,' said Fritz. Then to his brother, he whispered, 'The disease has already affected her mind.' Their mother smiled wistfully. 'I remember now,' she said. 'He's gone to wash for dinner.'

"Fritz manfully choked back his tears. 'That's right,' he said. 'Oh, Hans, yet we can hope. We must do everything in our power to help Papa save Mummy.' 'There's only one way I know of,' said Hans. He exchanged a knowing look with his brother, who nodded solemnly.

"And so it was that the next morning, Hans and Fritz secretly ripped out a corner of a page from the newspaper and set off in search of Diabolicus."

"Who's that?" Howie asked.

"Dr. Emil Alphonse Diabolicus," Chester went on to explain, "was the subject of talk and the object of fear in the town of Kasha-Varnishkes. He lived in an ancestral home, a decaying castle high upon a mountain bluff, and was never seen by day and only rarely by night. Some said he was a mad doctor, engaged in research, playing God. Others called him the devil's apprentice. But no one knew for certain what went on in the castle on the bluff. His housekeeper, who came into town each week to buy food, didn't engage in idle conversation. And none of the peasants were brave enough to venture up the mountainside to find out the truth for themselves. In fact, were it not for an unassuming little ad in the local paper, Hans and Fritz would never have known about the moneymaking opportunity they were about to pursue.

" 'Top bucks for research assistants,' the ad read. 'Inquire at The House of Dr.E.A.D.' "

I shuddered. "The House of Dread?" I asked Chester.

"The house of *Dr. Emil Alphonse Diabolicus*,"
he replied. "It was Hans whose hands lifted the
heavy knocker on the door, for once there, Fritz
was ready to turn back. 'Courage,' Hans said as
the door creaked open. With the eyes of an eagle
and the nose of a hawk, the housekeeper looked
down at the boys.

" 'What do you want?' she said.

" 'We . . . we've come about the ad,' said Hans.
There was a roll of thunder, even though it was a
sunny day.

" 'Thank the powers-that-be!' the old woman
exclaimed, clutching her withered hands to her
chest. 'You've arrived just in time. Come in, lads,
come in.'

"She put Hans and Fritz to work that very
afternoon, and they continued to work each afternoon for the next two weeks. But in all that time
they never met Dr. Diabolicus. They followed the
instructions of the housekeeper, who called herself
Erda, and were paid promptly at the end of each
day when they delivered to her what it was they
had been sent out to find."

"What?" Dawg said. "What were they sent out to find?" I noticed that he seemed more wide awake than ever. I was beginning to wonder if Chester's little story would put him to sleep by midnight. But I confess I almost didn't care. I wanted to hear the rest of the tale myself.

"Yeah, Chester," I said. "What were they looking for?"

A twinkle came into Chester's eyes. "Rabbits," he said.

"Rabbits!" Howie exclaimed. "What did he want rabbits for?"

"That was just what Hans and Fritz were asking themselves. It seemed that Dr. Diabolicus couldn't get enough rabbits. 'The ad in the paper said "research assistants," ' Hans pointed out one day. 'So he must be using the bunnies for research. But what *kind* of research?' 'Oh,' said Fritz, 'I don't want to know. We're getting paid, isn't that enough? We'll soon have the money to buy our passage to London, that's all that matters.'

"But it wasn't all that mattered to Hans. He had always been a more curious child than Fritz.

Two weeks of collecting rabbits for an unseen employer had proved more than he could take. He *had* to know what happened to the rabbits once they reached the House of Dr.E.A.D. Even more pressing was his desire to see the mysterious Dr. Diabolicus for himself.

" 'Perhaps,' he said, trying to reason with his brother, 'if we were to meet Diabolicus, we could convince him to let us help in other ways. Then, we'd not only have the money to get to London but to return home as well.'

"Well, it was hard for Fritz to argue with that kind of logic, especially since their mother's illness was progressing rapidly. Just the night before, she had boiled a sheepskin coat and called it mutton stew. The guests had not been amused. The brothers agreed that that night, they would find a way to sneak into the castle and speak with Dr. Diabolicus directly.

"Little did they know that the citizens of Kasha-Varnishkes had plans of their own for that evening, plans that would forever alter the destinies of the Transylvanian twins."

An owl hooted, eerily punctuating the pause in Chester's narrative. The night had become still, the air heavy. "What happened next?" Howie said, his voice sandpapery with fatigue. "Did Hans and Fritz find out why Diabolicus wanted the rabbits?"

"Oh, they found out, all right," said Chester. "Would that they hadn't. But Hans could not contain his curiosity."

"Sounds like someone I know," I muttered, thinking of all the trouble Chester's curiosity had gotten me into at one time or another.

Chester gave me a look but chose not to respond. "Late that afternoon, they delivered the day's catch as usual," he continued. "But instead of leaving immediately for home they asked Erda if they could each have a glass of milk. Before answering them, she glanced at the window. 'Well, all right,' she said. 'But you'll have to hurry. It's almost dark.' 'That's okay,' said Hans. 'We know our way home.' 'That isn't what worries me,' said Erda, and she went off to the kitchen.

"The moment she had left the room, Hans and Fritz raced quickly up the winding staircase that led to the upper floors of the house. Fritz clutched his brother's shirttail as they inched their way along the dark hall on the second level. 'Where are we going?' Fritz asked nervously. 'There,' said Hans, pointing to a pool of light spilling out from under a door at the far end of the hall. He hurried Fritz along, not wanting to be found out by the housekeeper.

"Despite its heaviness, the door opened easily and soundlessly on well-oiled hinges. The boys were not surprised by what they found inside. The candlelit laboratory was filled with buzzing machines, bubbling beakers, ticking clocks, and rabbits. Cages and cages and cages of rabbits.

" 'At least we know they're alive,' Hans said.

" 'Alive and yet not alive,' said a voice as well-oiled as the door.

"It was then that the boys met Dr. Diabolicus. He stood in the doorway, his pale face a shroud of skin on ancient bones, his lips red with life like overripe berries. He wore a silk robe, black as night with a silver moon and star embroidered on the breast pocket. In his white hands he carried two glasses of milk. 'These are yours, I believe,' he said, extending them toward the boys.

" 'Th-thank you, sir,' said Hans, stepping forward. He tried not to show his fear, while Fritz was failing miserably behind him. 'Won't you join us?'

" 'I don't drink . . . milk,' said Diabolicus.

"Hans' hands shook as he reached for the glass. 'Don't be frightened,' Diabolicus said. 'I'm not angry with you.'

" 'You're not?' said Fritz.

" 'Not at all. Without your help, I would have been unable to complete my experiments.' His eyes gleamed as he looked about the room. 'These rabbits are all evidence of my success,' he said. 'They are, like me, alive—yet not alive.' Hans and Fritz looked at each other, wondering what it was he meant by that phrase. 'I have been so lonely, boys,' said Diabolicus. 'But now my lonely days are over!' Opening a cage, he removed a pair of rabbits, white with black markings on their backs. 'Bella,' he said. 'And Boris. These are my special ones. They will accompany me through eternity and be my friends, my soulmates, always. You can understand how much pets mean to someone as lonely as I, can't you, lads?' "

I don't know about Howie and Dawg, but I got a little teary at that.

" 'Wherever I go,' Diabolicus continued, 'Bella and Boris shall go with me. And they will never die . . . never, never.'

"Hans started to ask how this could be, when the sound of pounding footsteps drove the thought from his mind. 'Hurry,' the housekeeper cried, as she broke into the room. 'Hurry, master! They're coming!'

" 'Get hold of yourself, woman! Who's coming?'

" 'The peasants. They're carrying torches. They're crying, "The monster must be destroyed!" Oh, master, we must leave at once.'

" 'The fools,' said Diabolicus. 'Don't they realize it is Saint George's Eve, the one night of the year I *can't* be destroyed?'

" 'But the rabbits,' said the housekeeper. 'You don't know for certain about the rabbits. They

could be destroyed. All your research, all your work ... all for nothing!'

"Diabolicus looked wildly about the room. 'You're right,' he said. 'But we haven't time to save them all.' He hugged Bella and Boris to him. 'I'll take these two. They shall be the parents of a new breed! Come, we must flee at once! What good fortune that my cousin is no longer using his home in London. Quickly, to the secret tunnel!'

"Without a moment's hesitation, Hans said. 'May we go with you, sir?'

"Fritz grabbed his brother's arm, too shocked to utter a sound. As the noises of the gathering crowd grew louder and louder outside the walls of the castle, Diabolicus considered the lad's request. 'I don't see why not,' he said, after a while. 'We'll be a family,' he said. 'A family . . . forever. Follow me!'

"As the boys ran after Dr. Diabolicus and his housekeeper, Fritz whispered hoarsely to his brother, 'Are you crazy? What's gotten into you?'

'I'm not crazy at all,' said Hans. 'We're going to London.'

"Yes, thought Fritz, as he boarded the black coach drawn by the black horses. We're going to London. But will we return?"

The moon was now high in the sky. It would soon be midnight. And Dawg was wide awake.

SEVEN

A Family Forever

"DID THEY EVER GET to London, Pop?" Howie asked.

"Eventually," Chester replied. "First, they had to make the arduous journey through Hungary and Austria, Switzerland and France. In each land, Bella and Boris met other rabbits, and in time their numbers grew."

"Gee," said Howie, "I'll bet I know where they found rabbits in France."

"Where?" Chester said.

"The hutch back of Notre Dame."

Howie got quite a chuckle out of this. Chester, I could see, was annoyed not to have his story taken seriously.

"And if they weren't there," Howie went on, "they could always have checked the Sor-bunny!" He laughed even harder, while a vacancy sign went up in Dawg's eyes.

Chester's tail began flicking the ground again. "If you don't want me to go on," he said.

"No, no!" Howie cried.

"Don't stop," said Dawg. "We've gotta know what happens next."

"Well," said Chester, relaxing his tail. "If you insist. Where was I?"

"France," said Howie, stifling a chuckle. "The hutch back—"

"Never mind that," said Chester. "After France, they crossed the English Channel and came at last to London, where they settled into Renfield Manor, their wearisome journey at its end.

" 'Sleep well, my children,' Diabolicus said to Hans and Fritz that first night, as the boys settled into two large feather beds in a tower bedroom. Hans and Fritz were so overcome with exhaustion from their travels, they barely heard the door close as Diabolicus slipped out of the room. But the sound of a heavy bolt falling into place jolted them awake.

" 'We're locked in,' Fritz whispered in alarm. 'I told you we shouldn't have spoken so freely on our way here. He knows we plan to leave him, Hans.'

" 'How could he have heard?' Hans said. 'We talked of our plans only during the day when he was sleeping in that crazy box of his. Boy, what a nut case he is.'

" 'Yeah? What about Erda?' said Fritz. 'She's as weird as he is. And those rabbits with their red eyes! Have you noticed their teeth, Hans? Have you seen how they've grown?'

" 'Don't worry,' Hans assured his brother. 'We'll be out of here tomorrow, mark my words. Tomorrow, we will be free.' And soon the two boys fell asleep.

"They didn't know that all this while Dr. Diabolicus had been listening outside their door. He didn't move, even now as they began to snore. 'Listen to them,' he said to the housekeeper, as she approached on slippered feet, 'the children of the night. What music they make. Ah, but Erda, they are deserting me. How can I let them go? They are my family, they are my *own*.'

" 'Give them eternal life,' Erda suggested.

" 'Eternal life?' said Diabolicus.

" 'You have given it to Bella and Boris. They will be with you always. Why not Hans and Fritz as well?'

" 'I don't have the time,' Diabolicus replied. 'It will take months to duplicate the laboratory I had in Transylvania. By then, the boys will be gone. Or if I manage to keep them here, it will only be by force, and they will hate me for being their jailer. No, Erda, they must be free—free to live and die. Free to leave me, as one day so shall you.' He turned with a heavy heart and went into the library, where he spent the night reading.

"Now it was his good fortune—and the ill fortune of Hans and Fritz—that one of the books he found on the dusty shelves that night was his cousin's diary. As he turned its pages, Diabolicus made the amazing discovery that he was not alone, after all! There were others like him. He was one of a breed of creatures known as vampires. And vampires, he learned, had ways of creating others of their kind. 'I don't need a laboratory,' Diabolicus said, laying the book on the table beside him. He licked his lips and ran his tongue over the two pointed teeth that hung like daggers inside his mouth. 'Everything I need is right here. It has been here all the time!' Slowly, he rose from his chair and climbed the staircase to the boys' bedroom."

There were sounds of twigs snapping and leaves crackling in the woods around me. I felt sure that Diabolicus was coming closer. Closer. I looked across at Howie and Dawg. Their eyes told me they felt as I did. Chester, seeing his effect on us, smiled contentedly.

"By morning," he said, "the boys were his."

"But how?" Howie asked. "What do you mean?"

"And what does this have to do with the rabbit?" said Dawg. "What'd ya say his name was? Binoculars?"

"Bunnicula," Chester said. "Oh, I'm coming to that, don't worry. Diabolicus had succeeded in turning Fritz and Hans, and then Erda too, into vampires like himself. He now had a wife, of sorts. And sons. And pets. His happiness, like his family, was complete.

"Fritz and Hans thought of Diabolicus and Erda as their father and mother. Their real parents were soon forgotten.

"Bella and Boris, being rabbits, increased their master's happiness by adding to the family. For some reason, they had an unusually small litter— a litter, in fact, of one. Noboby knew what to call this new member of the family. Bella and Boris seemed almost embarrassed to have produced such a runty thing as their sole offspring. And Diabolicus wondered just what sort of race he had created if this was the best they could manage. He did not know that Bella and Boris had already bred others of their kind throughout Europe; nor, that no sooner had they added to their numbers, than those very numbers had been cut down.

"You see, when Fritz and Hans disappeared from Kasha-Varnishkes, it was believed that they had perished in the fire that had destroyed The

House of Dr.E.A.D. But the boys' parents would not give up hope that they had survived. 'I will live to see my sons again,' their mother had proclaimed. And so her husband, together with several other men from the village, set out on the trail of Diabolicus and the black carriage.

"They followed them across Hungary and Austria, through Switzerland and France, and wherever they encountered the race of rabbits Bella and Boris had left behind, they destroyed them. By the time the men arrived on England's shores, there were no vampire rabbits left . . . none, that is, but Bella, Boris and the little one without a name.

"One night, shortly before dawn, Diabolicus was reading a bedtime story to Hans and Fritz. Hans held the tiny rabbit in his lap, stroking its head as he listened to his new father's voice. Suddenly, they heard Erda's footsteps racing madly up the stairs. 'Hurry,' she cried out breathlessly. 'Hurry, master! They're coming!'

" 'Get hold of yourself, woman,' said Diabolicus. 'Who's coming?'

" 'The peasants from Kasha-Varnishkes. They're carrying torches. They're crying, "The monster must be destroyed!" Oh, master, we must leave at once.'

"With a sense of *déjà vu*, Diabolicus ran to get Bella and Boris, while hurrying the boys and Erda to the carriage behind the house. 'Once it is daylight and we are asleep in our boxes of dirt,' he said, 'the horses will know where to carry us.'

"Their escape plan seemed perfect. But just as they were about to depart, Boris leaped from his master's arms and scampered back to the house. Diabolicus ran after him.

" 'Where are you going, Papa?' cried Fritz. 'We can't leave without you.' "

"Still a wimp," Dawg commented.

" 'I shall return,' Diabolicus called out. He chased Boris through an open door and was gone from sight.

"Now, whether Diabolicus ever reached Boris we will never know, for no sooner had he set foot in the house than it erupted in flames.

"The innkeeper from Kasha-Varnishkes wiped

a tear from his eye, convinced that his sons were now lost to him forever. And, of course, they were . . . just not in the way he thought. Had he turned away from the blazing carnage, he would have seen a black carriage disappearing into the forest. Two boys, one clutching a tiny rabbit, were taking a last look at their home, their England. They were headed for a new life, a new land. They were headed for America."

"America?" I said. "How'd they get to America?"

"Well, it just so happened," said Chester, "that Diabolicus had prepared for an emergency such as this one. He had booked passage under an assumed name on the *Q.E. II,* thus enabling Erda, Fritz, and Hans to board the ship one November night and never look back.

"They settled in their new country, keeping to themselves, always apart from the others. They saved wisely, invested in the stock market, and, in time, their cash flow was sufficient to allow them to construct a duplicate of their original home, an

American House of Dr.E.A.D. They lived a quiet life. And then one day their quiet life was destroyed.

"Bella and her baby rabbit escaped through an open window. We don't know what happened to Bella, but we know of course what became of the little one without a name."

"He came to live with a family called the Monroes," I said. "And they named him Bunnicula."

"Right."

"And The House of Dr.E.A.D.?" I asked.

Chester turned his head toward the house in the clearing. Three sets of eyes followed his. "You're looking at it," he said. "Fritz and Hans live there still, under other names, no doubt. Erda, though she is no longer called that, is their housekeeper. And somewhere, high in a tower room, there is a laboratory, the mirror image of one in Kasha-Varnishkes. The Transylvania twins will one day continue the experiments begun by their adopted father. They are waiting, waiting for Bunnicula."

The night was still. No one spoke for the longest time. Then, Howie said, "A hare-raising tale, Pop."

Dawg started to chuckle, but his chuckle turned quickly to a snort, and the snort into a snore. He was sound asleep. Moments later, Howie was sleeping too.

"Now's our chance," Chester said. "If we're not too late, we may still be able to save the Monroes."

And those were the last words I heard.

EIGHT

Dawg Gone! (And That's Not All)

HOW WE MANAGED to sleep that night I will never know. It may have been from sheer exhaustion, or perhaps it was the terror instilled in us by Chester's words, but no sooner had he finished his story than sleep moved in quickly and efficiently, like a thief in the night, to rob us of our wakefulness. Even Chester slept, although

he confessed to me when he woke that he had not slept easily.

I knew what he meant. I have never had such nightmares.

In one, I was lost in a woods. From all around me, I heard rustling, scampering, someone—or something—moving about. Every time I ran toward the sounds, they would disappear and start

again from another part of the forest. I ran and
ran, first toward them, then away, never knowing
who or what was making them, always frightened
they would find me before I could find them.

It was a different sound that woke me shortly
before dawn—the sound of rain. I listened for a
time to its patter on the leaves above me, my brain
too foggy to make sense of where I was or why I
should be afraid. I just knew that I was getting
wet, and that I *was* afraid.

"What a night," I heard Chester say beside me.
"They were all around us, Harold."

"Who?" I said, yawning loudly.

"The spirits. Didn't you hear them?"

I thought for a moment. "I heard sounds," I
said. "Do you mean they could have been—"

"Of course," said Chester. " 'The fifth of May
is Saint George's Day. When midnight tolls, the
devil has sway.' "

"And while the cat's asleep, the dog runs away,"
I added.

"What do you mean?"

I nodded toward the spot where Howie and

Dawg had fallen asleep the night before. Howie was opening his eyes. He was alone.

"Dawg gone!" he exclaimed.

"Just as I thought," said Chester. "He merely pretended to sleep. Oh, what fools we've been. Why couldn't we have stayed awake!"

"What is it, Pop?" Howie asked, quickly on his feet and at our side. "Did Dawg do something wrong?"

"Not in your eyes, certainly," Chester replied. He too was on his feet now, pacing nervously. "It all fits into place, just as I suspected. Harold, get up."

I stretched lazily. "Do I have to?" I asked.

"Do you ever want to see your family again?" he retorted. "Alive?"

I bounded to my feet. "Is it Bud and Spud?" I asked nervously. "Have they done something to the Monroes?"

Howie started to sniffle. "Maybe they know about Bunnicula," he said. "Maybe they've kidnapped the Monroes to force them to give back Bunnicula!"

"I think you're confusing things," I told Howie. "It was Fritz and Hans who wanted Bunnicula, not Bud and Spud. Besides, that story was make-believe."

"Hah!" "Hah!" Chester snorted. "Woe unto you who believeth not."

"On the contrary," I said. "Woe unto me who has believethed you too many times. How could that story be real, Chester? And where did you hear it in the first place?"

Chester paused long enough to bathe a paw. An evasive tactic, if ever I'd seen one. "My sources are confidential," he said at last. It was my turn to snort. "Besides, that story doesn't matter right now. What matters is the fate of the Monroes. I believe that Bud and Spud and Dawg were the evil spirits in these woods last night. I believe that Dawg purposely got us lost and wore us out so we'd be out of his masters' way all night. I believe that Bud and Spud had harmful intentions regarding the Monroes. I believe we may be too late."

"And woe until you who believeth not, Uncle Harold," said Howie, beginning to cry in earnest.

I confess I felt my own eyes dampening. "I hope for all our sakes that you're wrong, Chester," I said. "Otherwise, we'll . . . we'll be orphans. And I'm too old to be an orphan!"

"We have to get back to camp, Harold," Chester said. "Now!"

"There's only one problem," I said.

"What's that?"

"It's pouring." The drenched leaves above our heads were no longer protecting us. Even though I've never cared for the smell of wet dog hair, it wasn't that that concerned me as much as the difficulty of tracking in the rain. "If Dawg went back to camp," I told Chester, "I would ordinarily be able to follow his scent. But I'm afraid this fresh rain has wiped out that possibility."

"Rats," Chester muttered. "Well, we'll just have to find our way back as best we can."

We were all set to start out when Howie cried, "Look, Uncle Harold! Look, Pop! He's back!"

There, winding his way through the trees in our direction, was Dawg.

"DID YOU HEAR all the commotion?" he asked when he reached us. "I tried to follow it, but the ground was too wet and I lost the trail. Boy, the rain's been coming down for hours. You guys woulda slept through anything."

"And probably did," said Chester, under his breath. "You been up long, Dawg?" he asked.

"A couple hours. Chester, did you know you whistle when you sleep?"

Seeing the look in Chester's eye, I jumped in before he could respond. "Uh, the longer we stand here," I pointed out, "the wetter we get. How about taking us back to camp, Dawg?"

"That's just what I was going to do," said Dawg. "I was about to wake you, but then I heard the noise and took off after it. Like I say, I lost it."

Chester regarded Dawg suspiciously. "Have you lost your memory concerning the whereabouts of camp as well?"

"Nah. It's just down through the woods apiece. You fellas all set to head back?"

"How interesting," said Chester, "that you know the way so clearly this morning when you couldn't have found it last night to save your life. Or anybody else's."

Dawg gave Chester a puzzled look. "I wasn't trying to find camp last night," he said. "I was trying to find the house. I got lost. Don't you believe me?"

Chester said nothing.

Dawg's puzzled look was replaced by one of admiration. "You know, Chester," he said, "that was some story you told last night. It really scared me. I mean it put me to sleep and all. But did I have dreams!" The scar on his jowl glistened as he turned to lead us back to camp.

Dreams played on my mind as I followed along. We had all heard sounds in the night. Were they real or were they nightmares? Were Chester's fears just dreams of an over-vivid imagination, or was it possible that the spirit of evil was a reality with different names—and three of those names were Bud, Spud and Dawg?

What would we find, I asked myself, when we returned to camp? The rain was letting up now. It was starting to get light. Would the Monroes be stirring in their tent, surprised and happy to see us coming home? Would Toby run out and throw his arms around my neck and tell me how he'd worried about me all night long? Would Mr. Monroe pat my head and scratch the spot between my ears? Would Mrs. Monroe wipe me down with a big, soft towel?

"There it is!" I heard Dawg call out. In the distance, I saw the campsite. And all my thoughts turned into dreams.

It was deserted. The Monroes were gone. And so were Bud and Spud.

We ran down the slope past the charred remains of a fire. The Monroes' tent, a tarp once held up by poles and clothesline, had collapsed and was now a muddy landscape of canvas peaks and puddled valleys. I sniffed beneath it and was overcome by the scent of wet rubber and mildew. I thought I detected the odor of Mr. Monroe's sour-balls (cherry, I think) and Pete's socks, as well, but those faint aromas were mere traces, shadows of another time darkening the doorways of my nasal passages.

"Boy, they sure must have left in a hurry," Howie said. His words were somewhat garbled by the piece of clothing he carried in his mouth. As he came closer, I recognized it as one of Toby's T-shirts.

"Where'd you find that?" I asked.

"Over by that log," Howie said, dropping the T-shirt. "And look, Uncle Harold, it's ripped."

Chester's eyes grew wide. "A struggle," he said.

"Nonsense," I said, not wanting to believe what my eyes were telling me. "The Monroes aren't here because . . . because . . . because they're somewhere else."

"I love your mind, Harold," said Chester. "Let's take that logic a little further, shall we? Their tent is collapsed, their belongings are strewn about the place, their clothes are torn, everywhere you look there's—"

"Blood!"

Chester and I jerked our heads to see Howie staring down at the ground. "Blood, Pop," he said. "Uncle Harold, blood!" Could the pool at our feet really be what it seemed? Our eyes followed the reddish trail that led off into the woods.

We looked back at each other, too stunned to speak.

"I know where they are," a voice said. It was Dawg. In all the excitement, we'd forgotten all about him. "I know where they are," he repeated. "Follow me."

Chester and I regarded each other uncertainly. How did Dawg know where the Monroes had gone, unless Bud and Spud were with them? If we followed him, where would he take us? If we didn't follow him, would we ever see home—or the Monroes—again?

And, in the end, what choice did we have?

NINE

Trail's End

TRAILING DAWG, we wound our way along a well-worn path among the trees. It was barely raining now; the sun was beginning to shine through the clouds. Every few steps we would find another pool of water tinted pinkish-red. Even though the faint odor wasn't exactly bloodlike, we knew we were on a trail of evil. We just didn't know where it would lead.

Howie, as usual, was well ahead of us. Suddenly, he called out, "Pop, don't come any closer! Stay where you are!"

Chester arched his back, his hair rising straight and tall like a Mohawk Indian's. I suppose I should have been alarmed, too, but there was something about Howie's warning only Chester that made me brave enough to run ahead.

Howie stood beside an empty bottle. Dawg was sniffing at it. "Uncle Harold," Howie whined, "the blood ends here. Pop isn't safe. They're going to make him into . . . into soup!"

"Soup?" I said. I was completely at a loss as to what he meant until I read the label. "Catsup," I read aloud, though of course I pronounced it "ketchup."

"That doesn't say *cat soup?*" Howie asked, surprised.

Chester was now close enough to hear our conversation. "And there we have it, ladies and gentlemen," he said. "Further evidence of the damage to the brain caused by chewing on bones and chasing sticks."

"I believe," Dawg said, "that yer friend is making a crack about dogs." He growled.

I was about to step in, when Howie yipped loudly. "Pop!" he said. "Dawg! Uncle Harold, wait a minute! I don't understand. If the trail of blood—"

"Ketchup," Chester interjected.

"Whatever," said Howie. "If it doesn't lead to this bottle, then where *does* it lead?"

"There," Dawg said matter-of-factly, forgetting his anger toward Chester. We looked ahead, and in a clearing was the house from the night before. It seemed less forbidding by day, but I couldn't help remembering Chester's name for it—an American House of Dr.E.A.D.

"You've brought us full circle," I said. I was beginning to believe that there really was something to Chester's suspicions. "Why?"

"Because that's where you'll find Bud and Spud," Dawg said. "And if I'm not mistaken, you'll find your family there, too."

"What are they *doing* there?" Howie asked Dawg.

"Well, if it's Bud and Spud you mean," said Dawg, "they live there. As for yer kin, I couldn't say. All I know is this is where the trail is leading us."

Chester eyed Dawg coolly, doing a pretty fair imitation of Humphrey Bogart on the late show.

"So," he said, in a low voice, "if Bud and Spud live there, that means you live there, too." Dawg nodded, the ribbon of drool bobbing up and down with his head. "Why didn't you tell us that last night?"

Dawg shrugged. "You were so shook up by the place," he said, "I didn't have a chance. Besides, I liked yer story better'n the truth. Listen fellas, it looks like it's gonna start comin' down again. What'd ya say we move this conversation indoors?"

Somewhat reluctantly, we agreed. "A trap," Chester muttered as we crossed the clearing and drew nearer to the house. "We're doomed, Harold. Have you any last words?"

"When's breakfast?" I said, taking hope from the light in what looked to be a kitchen.

Dawg headed in that direction and scratched at the back door. I heard footsteps. They sounded familiar. Like those of. . . .

"Erda!" Chester squealed, as the door opened and an eagle-eyed, hawk-nosed woman peered down at us. "The housekeeper, Harold. My worst fantasies are coming true. Bud and Spud are really Fritz and Hans. There's a laboratory somewhere, a laboratory where experiments are done on innocent, little——"

Before he could finish his sentence, the woman at the door grabbed him up into her arms and held him tight. "Nice kitty," she said. "Why, Teufel, who've you brought home? Oh, I know, these must be our guests' lost pets. Now, won't they be happy to see you?"

Chester looked at me wildly. "Bark," he hissed.

"Oh, Chester, you know how I feel about——"

"Unless you have something better to do this morning than live, Harold, bark!"

"Well, since you put it that way," I said, and set about woofing for everything I was worth.

Howie joined in with some high-pitched yips of his own. Without thinking, the woman put her hands to her ears, and in so doing dropped Chester to the ground. He lost no time in bolting for the door, but found it closed. "No escape," he snapped. Dawg, meanwhile, just sat back and watched as if the three of us had gone completely mad.

"Stop this!" the woman cried. "Stop this racket at once, hear? You'll raise the dead!"

"Too late for that," Chester cracked and started for a door leading to the rest of the house. Howie and I ran after him, barking all the while, only to be stopped by the shadow that fell across the threshhold of the room.

"What's all the fuss?" said a voice I recognized as Bud's. I looked up and saw that he was rubbing sleep from his eyes.

Chester tried to squeeze between Bud's legs and the doorjamb, but Bud moved just in time to catch him in the ribs. "Now, hold on there, cat," he said, "where do you think you're going? Why's everybody in such a uproar this mornin'?"

"I think they're jes worked up over bein' out in the rain all night," the woman said. "Ain't that so, critters? I'll give 'em all some breakfast and you go on upstairs and finish yer sleepin'."

I saw Chester twitching to be free. When his

struggles got him nowhere, he sighed heavily and dropped his head. Bud reached down and picked him up. "Nah," he said. "I hear the others comin'. Why don't we all have breakfast?" He carried Chester to the kitchen table and sat down.

"Well," Chester said, over Bud's elbow, "you're getting your last request."

I felt my eyes tearing up again. "I guess breakfast isn't so important," I said. "What I really wish is that I could see the Monroes."

"Looks like you're getting that wish, too, Uncle Harold," Howie said. "Here they come."

All at once the room was filled with people. Toby ran to me and threw his arms around my neck just as I'd imagined only an hour earlier. Mr. Monroe patted me, then scratched me between the ears. Mrs. Monroe cooed at Howie, and Pete ignored us all. It was almost like being home. Almost . . . except for the strange woman with the eagle eyes, the scar-faced dog, the man at the table who wouldn't let Chester go, and the other man at the door who even at six o'clock in the morning was fondling a knife.

The woman began to busy herself at the refrigerator. "How about some milk, folks?"

"I don't drink milk," Bud said. Chester and I exchanged worried glances.

"Now how are you going to grow up to be big and strong if you don't drink your milk?" the woman said. "Your brother drinks it all the time, and look at him."

Spud flexed a muscle.

"I'm so glad the animals are safe," Mrs. Monroe said. She took Chester from Bud and petted him gently. "I was so worried I hardly slept."

"Well, I told ya Dawg knew his way around here," said Bud. "I knew there was nothin' to worry about so long as they was with him."

"And fortunately we were with you," Mrs. Monroe said. "I can't thank you enough for taking us in out of that terrible storm, Bud."

The other woman shook her head. "I have ta laugh everytime I hear him called that," she said. "It isn't his right name, you know."

Chester jumped out of Mrs. Monroe's arms,

landing by my side. "This is it," he said. "Meet Fritz and Hans, the long-lost Transylvanian twins."

"No?" said Mrs. Monroe, brushing cat hairs off her borrowed robe.

"Nope. This here's Buford. And the other one is Spalding. They picked up those silly nicknames at college."

"College?" said Mr. Monroe.

"Well, shore," the woman replied. "My boys graduated cum-loudy. Buford here is a architect. Spalding practices law."

"And one of these days, he'll get it right!" Bud said with a loud guffaw. Spud crossed the room and whacked him one.

"Boys, boys," said the woman. "Let's set a good example for the young'uns." And she nodded to Toby and Pete.

"Sorry, Mama," Spud said, chagrined.

"We'll behave ourselves," said Bud. "Can I help ya out with breakfast?"

"Shore can, Buford. Why don't you set the

table? And, Spalding, put that knife to use for once and cut us some bread. Before anything else, however, I'd appreciate yer feeding these poor critters what've been out all night in the wet."

Five minutes later, we found ourselves eating chopped steak out of silver bowls. "There must be good money in architecture," I observed.

"Not if all his houses look like this one," said Chester.

"Well, in any event, so much for your evil spirits."

"Yeah, Pop," Howie said, "these folks are real nice. A little weird, maybe, but nice."

"Thanks," said Dawg, slurping thirstily at a bowl of Perrier. "I think so, too."

I had to admit that Bud and Spud did seem a lot less threatening in the light of day. As Howie said, they were definitely a little weird—eccentric, I guess you'd say—but they were far from evil.

"And the noises we heard last night?" Chester said, exercising his forehead muscles.

"Bud and Spud and the Monroes escaping from the rain," I said. "It's obvious, isn't it?"

"But weren't there noises before that?" said Chester. "Didn't we all hear noises throughout the night?"

"That was probably Bud and Spud," Dawg said. We looked to him for an explanation.

"Well, remember I told you that they were going out looking for something last night? They were going to find 'it,' remember? I don't know what 'it' is, but I'll bet that's what all the noise was about."

Just then, Bud, who had left the room while we were eating, appeared at the door with a cage in his hand. He held it high so that no one could see its contents.

"And now we have the answer," Chester said. "If it's a rabbit, you can bet these two clowns were named Fritz and Hans long before they were Buford and Spalding, *or* Bud and Spud."

"Mama," Bud announced, "this is for you. We was goin' to save it for Mother's Day, but we know how much you've wanted one. You keep such an eye out on us, we couldn't look during the day. We had to wait till a clear night to fetch one."

"Oh, now, Buford. Cut the preamble and just gimme! I'm dyin' from the suspense."

"Well, all right, Mama," said Bud, lowering the cage. "Here it is, then. It's all yers."

Everyone's eyes were on the cage as it came into view. I don't know about anyone else, but I was ready to see a rabbit there . . . a rabbit perhaps with fangs . . . a rabbit with red eyes. The last thing I was expecting was. . . .

"A baby skunk! Oh, boys, come here and let me give you a hug."

"Happy Mother's Day," said Bud.

The two sons dutifully kissed their mother's cheeks as she took the cage from them. "Well, hello, you little darlin'," she said to the thing in the cage. "We'll have to get you descented. But first you'll need a name. What am I going to call you?"

"Skunnicula?" I suggested to Chester.

"Ha. Ha. Very. Funny," he replied through gritted teeth. Then, mumbling something about "lunatics," he wandered off to a corner of the room, where he curled up for a nap.

"What's the matter?" I asked, joining him. "Suffering from post-Saint-George's-Day letdown?"

He grunted and shut his eyes. Soon Howie and Dawg were huddled in the corner with us, and we were feeling the warmth of the early morning sun as it poured in through a window. I was lost in my own thoughts about the night we'd just passed, a night full of adventures and dreams. It had been fun in a way; at least that's the way it seemed, now that it was over. It was scary being lost in the woods, but I realized that the greatest fears had been caused by my own imagination—that, and Chester's story, which I laughed now to think I had actually believed.

I picked up only snatches of the conversation in the room. I heard Pete asking for permission to call his friend Kyle . . . yes, so early in the morning because Kyle was going away for the rest of the day . . . and no, it couldn't wait, it was important, *really* important. I heard him talking in a hushed voice on the phone, then getting excited, then shouting: "It's happened! It's happened!" I heard his mother ask what all the commotion was about. And then I heard him say something about rabbits.

My eyes opened first. Then Chester's. Then Howie's. And finally Dawg's. We all listened as Pete explained his phone call.

"It's my other merit badge project," he was saying. "The secret one. Kyle bought a rabbit, see. And I've been taking Bunnicula over to his house, and, well, we're going to get badges in rabbit raising. And last night they had their first fryers, that's what you call the babies, see, and one of them . . . this is the best part, it's so cool . . . one of the little boy bunnies looks just like Bunnicula!"

Chester's eyes glazed over. He didn't move. And for the first time since I've known him, which is a long, long time, he was speechless.

"Pop looks sick," Howie said. "Better bring the cat a tonic."

"I don't think it's medicine Chester needs," I said. "I think it's a vacation."

"Looks like his brain's started out on one without him," said Dawg.

"I thought we were *on* a vacation, Uncle Harold," Howie said. "It's been fun, hasn't it? Even the scary part, right?"

I nodded and started to drift off to sleep. It hadn't been such a bad vacation, really. There was only one thing missing. Right then, I couldn't place it. But then the smell woke me and I remembered.

S'mores. Fresh from the microwave.

Toby gave me the first one out. Good old Toby. As I chewed contentedly, the Monroes began to sing.

" 'Someone's in the kitchen with Dinah, someone's in the kitchen I know-oh-oh-oh.' "

Howie, Dawg, and I howled along. And everyone was happy.

Everyone but Chester, that is. He hadn't left his spot in the corner. His eyes were staring off into space. His lips were moving, but not in rhythm to the song. It wasn't until we stopped singing that I caught a few words, and even then I wasn't sure what to make of them.

Perhaps you, dear reader, will know what he meant when he said, "When the moon comes out on Saint George's Day, the son also rises. *And he's here to stay!*"

I HAVE TAKEN LICENSE with the date of Saint George's Day, a holiday observed in England on April 23. My source—and Chester's—is Bram Stoker's famous novel, *Dracula*, which gives the date as May 5.

Harold X.

The bunny's back!

Here's a look at the next Bunnicula adventure,

[ONE]

The Omen

IT was the third straight day of rain. The
third day of listening to Mr. Monroe whistle
the score of *The Phantom of the Opera* through
his teeth while indexing his collection of meat-
less soup recipes. The third day of Mrs. Monroe's saying, increasingly less cheerfully,
"Channel Six says it's going to clear by morning." The third day of Pete whining about
what a rotten summer it had been and Toby
asking When was it going to stop because how
could he try his new skateboard? and Were
they going to go on vacation even if it kept

raining? and Why couldn't they ever rent the movies *he* wanted at the video store?

Not that the Monroes were the only ones getting, shall we say, edgy. No, even we pets—we who ordinarily exemplify a calm acceptance of fate to which humans can merely aspire—even we were losing it. My first inkling of this came when I found Howie racing around the basement on his little dachshund legs going, "Vroom, vroom."

"Uh, Howie, what are you doing?" I asked.

"It's the challenge of my career, Uncle Harold," Howie panted excitedly. "I'm chasing hubcaps at the Indianapolis Five Hundred."

I would have had a little reality chat with Howie then and there if I hadn't caught myself that very morning gazing into the mirror on Mrs. Monroe's closet door and wondering if the time hadn't come for me to try something different with my hair.

Even Bunnicula, usually the calmest of us all, had taken to hopping around his cage as if the floor were covered with hot tar and twitching his nose so rapidly you would have thought he'd suffer from whisker burnout.

Surprisingly, only Chester seemed unaffected by the elements. Or perhaps I should say that if he was affected, it was not in the way one would have anticipated. As the rest of us grew more irritable, Chester mellowed.

"How do you do it?" I moaned on the third night, as the rain continued to pelt the windows and I tried in vain to find an acceptable spot for settling down to sleep. At this point, every square inch of carpet looked the same and I was desperate for a change. Chester, meanwhile, was curled up happily shedding on his favorite brown velvet armchair, an open book in front of him and a contented-on-its-way-to-becoming-smug smile on his face.

"Why aren't you going crazy like everybody else?" I demanded. "What's your secret?"

His smile grew more knowing. "Books," he said, with a nod to the one in front of him, "are not only windows to the world, dear Harold, they are pathways to inner peace."

I shook my head. "I've tried books," I said. "Fifteen minutes and all I ended up with was cardboard breath."

"Try reading them instead of chewing them," Chester advised.

"Oh." This hadn't occurred to me.

Chester is a big reader. The problem is that his reading often gets us into trouble—especially considering the *kinds* of books he likes to read.

"So what are you reading about now?" I asked. "The supernatural?"

"The paranormal," he said.

"Well, that's a relief. Pair of normal what?"

"No, Harold, not a 'pair of normal,' the *paranormal*. How shall I explain this? The paranormal are experiences that are . . . . beyond explanation. Like Bunnicula, for example."

Chester believes our little bunny is a vampire.

"Or Howie."

"Howie?"

"I'm still convinced he's part werewolf. That's no ordinary howl on that dog."

"Uh-huh," I said.

"Or," Chester went on, if I may use the expression with regard to a cat, doggedly, "haven't you ever felt that something was about to happen, you just knew it in your bones, and then, bam! it happened?"

A chill ran down my spine. "Chester!" I cried. "I had a paranormal experience just the other night."

Chester's eyes lit up. "Really? Tell me about it, Harold."

"Well, it was after dinner and I was lying over there by the sofa, where Howie's sleeping now and . . . I was yawning and I felt my eyes growing heavy . . ."

"Yes? Go on."

"And I had this overpowering feeling that I was about to . . ."

"What, Harold? Oh, this is really exciting. Go ahead."

"That I was about to fall asleep. And I did."

Chester looked at me for a long time without speaking. "And do you have the feeling that you're about to experience pain?" he asked at last.

"You mean right now? Well, no."

The book fell off the chair. It landed on my paw.

"Ow!" I cried.

"Never discount the paranormal," were Chester's parting words, and he jumped down and headed toward the kitchen in search of a midnight snack.

I wanted to whimper but no one was around or awake enough to hear. This made me ask myself the question, If a tree falls on a dog in the forest, does the dog make a sound? I was eager to share this provocative conversation starter with Chester when my gaze fell on the open pages at my feet. I began to read.

Harriet M. of Niskayuna, New York, reports the fascinating case of the phantom telephone conversation. *"I had been talking with my sister*

Shirley for seventeen minutes late one afternoon before
I noticed that the phone plug was disconnected," she
writes. "The next day I told Shirley what had
happened and when. Stunned, she informed me that
she had had oral surgery just two hours prior to the
phantom conversation and her mouth was wired
shut. She would have been incapable of speaking to
me even if the phone had been hooked up!"

Incredibly, Harriet herself suffered such extreme
tooth pain the following day that she too was forced
to undergo emergency oral surgery. While under the
effects of anesthesia, she recalled her sister's words
during their nonexistent (??) conversation: "That
new dentist is so cute. I'd do anything to see him,
wouldn't you?"

"Amazing stuff, isn't it?"

I looked up at the sound of Chester's voice
as he emerged from the kitchen, licking milk
from his lips. Now I understood how he'd re-
mained so calm all this time. His brain had
turned into a two-week-old banana days ago.

*   *   *

THE rain stopped at exactly three o'clock in the morning. I remember the time because I was awakened just before the clock in the hall chimed the hour. It was not the rain that woke me, however, nor the ticking of the clock. It was a voice.

"Harold," it whispered in my ear, "something terrible is going to happen."

Go away, I thought. But the voice persisted.

"Harold," it intoned. "Wake up."

I knew that voice. Who else would wake me in the middle of the night just to tell me something terrible was going to happen?

"What do you want, Chester?" I mumbled without opening my eyes.

"I've seen an omen." He was louder now that he knew he'd succeeded in awakening me. "Don't you want to see it?"

"That's okay," I said, yawning. "I'll wait for it to come out on video."

"Very funny. Come on, Harold, it's not every day you get to see an omen."

I was going to point out that it was night, not day, but I knew that the difference would be irrelevant to Chester.

Howie was awake now too. He raced over to join us. "I want to see an omen, Pop," he said to Chester. Howie, for unknown reasons, calls Chester "Pop". "What's an omen?"

"A sign that something terrible is going to happen," Chester replied.

Howie shook his head. "I've seen signs like that," he muttered. "NO DOGS ALLOWED. Don't you hate that one? And, oh, here's one that really means something terrible is going to happen: DON'T WALK, when the hydrant is on the other side of the street."

Chester pretended to ignore Howie. "Come on, you two," he said. Apparently, he was unimpressed by the fact that I had both my front paws over my face and was loudly snoring.

"Stop faking, Harold," he said, tapping my eyelids. "Open up. Let's go."

Much against my will, I followed Chester

and the relentlessly energetic Howie into the front hall. It was then that the clock struck three and the rain suddenly stopped.

"Look!" Chester commanded. "There, by the front door."

I looked, but I didn't see anything I'd call an omen. I told Chester so.

"Look again," was his response.

And then I saw it.

There, next to the umbrella stand, was Chester's cat carrier. It was open.

"What's that doing there?" I asked.

"And what does it mean?" said Howie.

I felt myself begin to quiver. "It resembles an open mouth," I sniveled. "It means . . . it means . . . we're all going to have oral surgery! Well, I'm not going! I don't care how cute the dentist is."

"Harold!" Chester snapped. "Nobody's having oral surgery."

"Oh. Well, that's a relief."

"But it does mean we're going somewhere and I don't think we're going to like it."

"Why do you say that?" I asked.

"'We would have heard about it if it was anything good. You know what the Monroes are like. They tell us everything. But no one has said a word, so it must be a place too . . . *horrible* . . . to talk about."

There was a scuffling sound in the living room. We turned. Bunnicula was hopping about nervously in his cage. His eyes glistened in the dark.

I ran to him. "Don't worry, little furry friend," I said. "Nothing terrible is going to happen."

"Mark my words," Chester said, "we are doomed."

Photos by Carol Royce-Wilder